THE KIDNAPPING OF Sr. Angelus

Wendy Elmer

authorHOUSE®

AuthorHouse™ LLC
1663 Liberty Drive
Bloomington, IN 47403
www.authorhouse.com
Phone: 1-800-839-8640

Published by AuthorHouse 05/08/2014

ISBN: 978-1-4969-1221-3 (sc)
ISBN: 978-1-4969-1220-6 (e)

CHAPTER 1

On Friday Oct. 24th, 2010 Sr. Angelus was in her office preparing a speech for an assembly scheduled for the following week Friday Oct. 31st. It was going to be a dos and don'ts of safety for trick or treating. She didn't want it to sound like a 10 Commandments lecture. She wanted it to be informative while not sounding boring. She had a knock on her door. It was her secretary. She announced that she had a visitor by the name of Sister Philomena. Poor Sister Angelus almost fell off the chair when she heard that. Sister Philomena happened to be the head provincial of the whole order. Sister Angelus said: "Show her in please." She tried to smile genuinely. Sister Philomena entered and she said: "Please sit down. This is not a formal visit."

Sister Angelus said: "It is a pleasure to see you. What brings you here to Las Vegas?"

Sister Philomena said; "I am doing my rounds of visiting my whole order. I heard you were the only one here in Las Vegas. I was wandering in the airport and looking at the departure board. Since I am still in the habit some people will go out of their way to help me out. I had the nerve to ask for a one way ticket to Las Vegas. He pulled out his credit card and escorted me to the gate. He spun a tale about me being his elderly aunt. I laughed all the way over here."

Sister Angelus asked: "Where did you fly in from?"

Sister Philomena said: "I think it was from Wisconsin, but I am so jet lagged I might be on Pluto and not know it."

Sister Angelus asked: "How long can you stay?"

Sister Philomena said: "I want to take a rest for a while."

Sister Angelus asked; "When you got off the plane how did you get here to St. Peters?"

Sister Philomena said: "I met a few cops at the airport. They flashed their guns and badges. They gave me a ride. They knew you."

Sister Angelus said: "I know that squad. They are former students of mine. Life separated us and God reunited us years later. I belong to a women's group consisting of their wives. I do need your help with one thing. I just found out my first grade teacher will be out for six months because of breast cancer. I need a substitute. Would you give it a shot?"

Sister Philomena said: "It would be my pleasure to do that. New I need just one thing from you. What I really want is a home cooked meal."

Sister Angelus said: "Within two days I can have at least 13 people assembled in Robert's house for a turkey dinner. Leave that to me."

Sister Philomena said: " My last adventure was trying to convince five teenagers to join the convent. Have you ever had any inquiries about being a nun?"

Sister Angelus said: "Actually I have. I set up a talk at the local high school at career day. Father Raaser tried to recruit the boys to become priests. Hey you never know where you will find the next one."

Sister Philomena said: "Good call Angelus. I never considered such a road. How many inquiries did you get?"

Sister Angelus said: "About ten girls stopped by. Maybe fifteen boys for Father Raaser. We had a deacon here last year. He thought he was doing a good thing and went to a local orphanage. He took all boys and presented them to Father Raaser. Here are your new vocations he said. I think it took him a week to put a whole sentence together. He meant well, but went about it the wrong way."

Sister Angelus walked Sr. Philomena over to the rectory. She wanted a nap to get caught up on the right time. Father Raaser welcomed them with open arms. Sr. Angelus returned to her office to call Robert and Joyce. Robert said to meet him outside the supermarket and give him $20.00 to buy the carrots. He did it all. Joyce gave him a shopping list. After Sister Philomena's nap she felt better. They ate dinner together in the rectory. The two nuns returned home after an evening of talking and eating cake. They went by way of the basement. The two of them retired to their chambers for an early bed time.

CHAPTER 2

On Sunday they gathered in church for Sunday Mass. They all sat together in the same pew. Joyce was the only one missing because she was home doing the cooking. She came to church on Saturday night. Robert said that dinner would be ready by 12:00, so please be there by 11:00 to socialize and get to know Sr. Philomena. That gave the two nuns time to go home and talk some more. They ended up watching TV instead. At 10:40 they left the convent and drove over to Robert's house. At 11:00 they rang the doorbell and Robert answered. Daisy the dog was right there to bark out a greeting. She started wagging her tail and yipping. Robert had to pull her off of the poor new visitor. Sister Philomena passed the Daisy inspection.

Robert said: "Sorry about that. She means you no harm by doing that."

Sister Philomena said: "She is adorable. Where did you get her from?"

Robert said: "My wife brought her home from work. A colleague of hers had a dog who got pregnant. Daisy picked out my wife to be her owner."

Joyce said: "I tried to introduce Robert to Daisy before they met. By this time Daisy was fully active. I gave her a pair of his shorts to sniff and she ran behind her mother and hid the rest of the day. When I brought her home she curled right up into my husband's lap with her snout pointing in "that area". They have been inseparable ever since."

Sister Philomena said: "Whatever you did she seems to be well trained."

Joyce said: "Let us adjourn to the kitchen. The gentlemen gather in the living room."

When they entered the kitchen all the ladies were already there fussing with the food. Poking the potatoes stirring the carrots, anything else they thought needed doing. They all stopped abruptly and introduced themselves. Sister Philomena already met the gentlemen a few hours earlier. Sister Philomena told them all about her work and her life as a Mother Superior. They all said that they didn't know any families with kids. Eloise said she had a daughter, but that she was only six years old. Just a tad it too young to be professed as a nun.

At precisely 12:00 noon everybody got the food onto the plates and brought everything into the dining room. Robert took care of the turkey. Everybody stood behind the chairs and Robert did the blessing. Then everybody sat down and the food was passed around. Sister Philomena was already informed of the dinner ritual at Robert's house.

Sister Angelus said: "So. Sister Philomena will be with us for the rest of the academic school year. I just found out that our first grade teacher will be out with breast cancer for six months."

Norman asked: "What about vocations? Do you get inquiries about joining when people find out that you are the provincial?"

Sister Philomena said: "Most people don't know what that means. I pretty much work with the nuns already professed. My assignment at one time was to put on a retreat for young women interested in the convent. Out of 20 girls 3 made it to profession. That was a jackpot hit in those days. After that I was promoted to head provincial. The good part about being head provincial is that I get to move around. If somebody is rude I can recommend that they get psychiatric help. They have a vow of obedience, so

I can throw that up in their face. People are usually on their best behavior with me in the house.

Robert asked: "How long have you been provincial?"

Sister Philomena said: "About five years now. I get to move around a lot."

John asked; "How did you end up in Las Vegas?"

Sister Philomena said: "I was at the airport reading the departure board. A stranger walked up to me and asked if I needed help. He went out of his way to buy me a ticked and walked me over to the gate. I was laughing all the way to Las Vegas. When I got off the plane I saw you fellows with your guns and badges showing."

John asked; "I noticed you are wearing the habit. Did that change after you were professed or before?"

Sister Philomena said: "That changed after I was professed. I thought people would respect me more if I still wore the habit. I was right. People do go out of their way for me. I ended up with a free trip to Las Vegas. How many other people can say that?"

Norman asked: "What does Father Raaser do on Sundays? We have never had him over for turkey dinners."

Sister Angelus said: "Nobody really knows. Every time I ask him he says he visits sick parishioners. He claims to do hospital calls. Nobody ever questions that answer."

Arlene asked: "Excuse me Sister Angelus. Is Sister Philomena going to be my new teacher?"

Sister Angelus said: "No. Sister Philomena will be substituting for the other first grade class. You will still have the same teacher."

At the end of the meal everybody followed the usual routine for the turkey dinner. The ladies adjourned to the living room while the gentlemen cleared the table. The two nuns took home the carrots. It was their favorite vegetable. The two nuns left early so they can prepare for tomorrow's lessons and figure out the students in class. Sister Angelus gave her the low down on the who's who of the kids. Luckily at the age there wasn't any problem with bullies yet. They went to bed early and got up early. She was as ready as she would ever be.

CHAPTER 3

On Monday morning Sister Angelus led the class into the classroom. It was a class of 24 children. 12 boys and 12 girls. They were assigned seats alphabetically from left to right. This made it easier to learn their names.

Sister Angelus said: "Good morning boys and girls. I hope you had a nice weekend. We have a substitute teacher for the rest of the year. Her name is Sister Philomena. I know you will give her the respect she deserves. With that I leave you in her hands."

At lunch time the two nuns met and kept their eyes on the kids.

Sister Angelus asked: "How is it going with the kids?"

Sister Philomena said: "It seems to be going fine. The kids are very curious about me. The first hour I had to answer questions from them. I patiently answered them. Then I gave them math homework of two pages. The kids are patiently telling me their next page. These kids down here are rather quiet and pensive."

Sister Angelus said: "This is because it is your first week. It is a fake start. By Easter you will be glad to be rid of them."

Sister Philomena said: "By the way. What time is the assembly of Friday?"

Sister Angelus said: "I figured 9:30. Be in the gym by 9:15. They can relax and talk to each other and get goofy for a few minutes. After lunch they will be all wired with excitement. I will announce that they will be allowed to wear their Halloween costumes to school. I want this to be a festive day for them. Don't give them any tests on that day." Sister Philomena agreed to do this.

CHAPTER 4

At 9:15 everybody was assembled in the classrooms covered in their Halloween costumes. There was a lot of giggling and talking. When Sr. Philomena got the class quieted down she was finally able to teach something. The original way kids went dressed up was to dress up as the saints they were named after. They didn't get candy, they got to preach to the adults the lives of the saints they were named after. It was the only night of the year that kids got away with preaching to grown ups. Sr. Philomena wasn't sure where the gym was. She followed the other 1st grade class. She didn't realize that until the last minute. Sister Angelus walked onto the stage and called attention to the assembly.

She started to say: "Good morning everyone. I see you are all dressed up in your costumes. Today I will give you reminders of safety. Always go in groups and never enter a home where you don't know the people answering the door." Just then 4 people came out of the blue. One threw a blanket over Sr. Angelus and the rest picked her up and dragged her out of the gym. They heard a car roar away. The children and teachers looked at each other in puzzlement. They thought Sr. Angelus was teaching them a lesson. Arlene picked up her cell phone and called her mother. Her mother called Robert at the precinct. Sister Philomena got up on stage and said: "Boys and girls. This is unplanned and I have no idea when Sister Angelus will return. In the meantime my class will be joining the other first grade class. I will act as substitute principal until she returns. Everyone please return to your classrooms for your regular classes. Teachers use the lesson plans you wrote out for the day." Everybody returned just as instructed.

CHAPTER 5

By the time Sister Philomena returned to the school office there was a screeching of tires and a wailing of sirens. Robert and Norman jumped out of the car practically before the car stopped. They stormed the school like gangbusters. John busted the door open and barked out orders to Sister Philomena.

John yelled: "What happened to Sister Angelus?!!!"

Norman said: "Calm down John. Screaming at people won't get you anywhere. Sister Philomena, I want the whole story. Everybody's reaction. What happened from the time you got up this morning until the time of the kidnapping?"

Sister Philomena yelled: "Don't you come in here like gang busters. Who do you think you are talking to? I am a nun after all!!"

John yelled back: "I don't give a hoot if you are Jesus Christ Himself!!! We need to know what happened! The sooner the better NOW WOMAN!!!"

Robert said: "Calm down everyone. Screaming fest is not getting the work done. We need to figure out how to solve this problem. Let's talk civilly for a while. Sister Philomena, please tell us what happened."

Sister Philomena said: "I apologize for yelling and losing it, but I am under pressure to get her back."

Norman said; "Sit down and try to think clearly. Has there been a ransom note yet?"

Sister Philomena said: "No. The phone hasn't rung yet. I don't know what I am doing yet. Somebody knocked on the door and Robert opened it. It turned out to be her secretary standing there holding cups of coffee and donuts.

Robert asked: "Did you get a look at the kidnappers?"

Sister Philomena said: "I confronted one of them with an AK47. It was a machine gun of sorts."

Norman said: "I am afraid to as, but what did you say to her?"

Sister Philomena said: "It was wearing something covered from head to toe. I couldn't swear that it was a man or a woman. She pointed the machine gun at me and I just lost composure. I grabbed the gun and threw it across the room. I threw it towards the exit. Away from the children. I need a lot of naughty words the children should not have heard. I just lost composure yet another time. I think I scared her too. She ran away like her pants were on fire. If I had a ruler in my hand I would have rapped her knuckles raw."

Norman said: "Okay kids. Here is the plan. Robert, stay here in case there is contact with the kidnappers. It has been our experience that people will kidnap people just to pay the rent. Sister. Philomena, you will return to the convent for the night. Father Raaser will sit by the phone in the rectory. John will sit with you all night. Robert will sleep here all night in case the phone rings. The rectory has a roll away bed. In the meantime go through her papers and see if you get a hint of who might have done this. Go through the files. There will be no gossip outside of this office. Joh, go to the convent now please. Jack, you call the rectory and inform Father Raaser of this development. I am going to stay in the rectory."

CHAPTER 6

Everybody went their separate ways and to the separate assignments. John was allowed to call his wife and stay in the convent for company. Michelle came over and brought dinner for all three of them. Sister Philomena was embarrassed about being waited on by a guest in the house. John told Sister Philomena that she should prepare the lessons for next week. The kidnapper wants to upset the apple cart. There was a ringing of the doorbell and Sister Philomena almost jumped through the roof. It turned out to be trick or treaters. She forgot all about it because of the events of the day. Luckily Michelle stopped off at the store and brought a few packages of mini chocolates. It was the variety kind. She brought one package of M&M's for themselves. Sister Philomena told her to make sure she looks through the peep hole before opening the door. John found a few plastic pumpkins around the convent.

John took them outside and tied them to the fence. This prevented the three of them from getting up every 5 minutes. Luckily for John Michelle remembered to bring him clean underwear for the night. At 9:00 everybody drifted off to sleep. Sister Philomena in her bed, John in the lounge chair, and Michelle on the couch. They were told not to enter Sr. Angelus' room. It was to remain untouched just as she left it. In the morning the three cops were going to go through it one thing at a time. Sister Philomena was warned ahead of time that it wasn't going to be pretty. Joyce was assigned the task of going through her drawers with her under things in it. They all promised there wouldn't be any jokes or impolite comments on her possessions.

CHAPTER 7

Father Raaser was beside himself when he heard what happened. He allowed Robert to stay at the rectory. The next day was All Saints Day, a Holy Day of Obligation for all Catholics. During the night Robert and Joyce revisited a case that occurred in the church a few years previous. They walked that route again. They searched every inch of the church. All the nooks and crannies that she could possibly be stored at. They came up with othing. They showered and went to bed early. Robert suggested that maybe something will come to them in their sleep. Father Raaser promised to wake up Robert the minute he thought of something. Before going to bed Robert made on last check of the locked doors of the church. He took the flashlight and flashed it around. He saw nothing, but go scared out of his wits. He flew back to the rectory like a flash. Robert slept on a roll away cot.

The next morning the two of them woke up early and still came up blank. They went to Mass after breakfast. Father Raaser did not mention the problem at Mass. He didn't want to scare off the kidnappers. He also looked suspiciously at each and every parishioner. At the end of the Mass all the squad gathered in the sacristy. They found Father Raaser turning white as a sheet. He yelled: "Norman, look at this!!!"

Norman said: "Calm down son. Don't touch that piece of paper. What does it say?"

John read it out loud. If you want to see Sr. Angelus again it will cost you $20,000.00. You will be contacted tonight at 6:00 in the rectory."

Norman asked: "Where would you get the ransom $20,000.00?"

John asked: "How much Is the tuition for St. Peter's School?"

Father Raaser said: "The tuition is $250.00 a month."

John's quick calculation revealed that $20,000.00 is how much tuition is paid from 1st to 8th grade. He said it was probably written by a disgruntled former student.

Norman said: "Good thinking John. Let's ride with it. Father Raaser, call the archdiocese and inform them of what is happening."

Two hours after that phone call the rectory doorbell rang and the archbishop himself was standing there with a briefcase full of cash money. It was the ransom money that was demanded.

Norman asked: "How did the ransom note get in here?"

Robert said: "We haven't figured that out yet sir. We were all at Mass. Nobody saw anybody enter or exit the sacristy. Maybe somebody came out of the back stairs and slipped out again. That would have to be somebody who knows the route."

Norman asked: "Who knows that route?"

Father Raaser said: "Former priests. That is all I know."

Robert said: "Archbishop sir. Please read the board nailed to the confessional. These are the names of the former priests who were transferred out of here. Verify their whereabouts and make sure they really were where they are supposed to be. They might respond faster to a call from you than a call from a cop."

The archbishop left to do the assignment.

CHAPTER 8

Two hours later Father Raaser returned to the rectory and reported that he personally verified the whereabouts of all the priests. They were cleared by the archbishop himself. When he arrived back at the rectory there were many more cars parked in the driveway. They had to open up the school yard for them to park. The cops brought the unmarked cars so they don't attract attention unnecessarily. They were busy enough as it was.

Sister Philomena asked: "What happens next?"

Norman said: "Officer Alex will bring you back to the convent. You will stay there until further notice. If you need groceries or anything Alex will call john on his cell phone. K-9 dog units did not yield where Sister Angelus was being held. She was definitely off the premises."

Officer Alex helped Sister Philomena up off the couch and led her to the front door. Her hands were icy cold. When they were outside Alex said: "Excuse me sister. Where is the convent?"

Sister Philomena pointed across the way and showed him where to go. When they arrived and got settled in Alex made a pot of tea. He couldn't find any sweets. Sr. Philomena asked: "Alex, are you also an alumnus of Sister Angelus and St. Peter's school?"

Officer Alex said: "No sister. I grew up in Eli, a town north of here. If you are still around I can take you up there in the summer. It is a rather picturesque small town. I brought Sr. Angelus there last summer for the weekend last year. She loved it."

Sister Philomena asked: "Will the police be interviewing the children?"

Officer Alex said: "I don't know. Tomorrow I will talk to Robert about that."

CHAPTER 9

At 3:00p.m. precisely the phone rang in the rectory. It was the kidnappers. It was a computer scrambled voice that sounded mechanical. The machines were able to set up throughout the rectory to trace the call. It was difficult because of the scrambled voice. Father Raaser was asked to keep the caller on the line as long as possible.

Father Raaser said: "St. Peter's may I help you?"

The caller said: "We have your nun Sister Angelus."

Father Raaser asked: "What do you want?"

The caller said: "$20,000.00 in cash delivered to the lamp post in the park."

Father Raaser asked: "Which lamp post?"

The caller said: "Enter on the north side of the park. Set the bag down at the base of the lamp post.

Use the second lamp post and don't bring the cops. Bring it at midnight tonight. Do not screw this up."

At midnight Father Raaser arrived without the cops. He put the paper bag down just as instructed. The cops were there dressed all in black. They were hiding unseen. Luckily they weren't noticed.

Father Raaser yelled out loud to the darkness: "You have the money. Where is Sister Angelus?"

The kidnapper came out from behind a tree and said: "Go and look for her. She isn't too hard to find. Very well done Father. You learned very well to take instructions from the seminary. Go home now. Walk towards that black unmarked car and don't look back."

What the kidnapper didn't know was that he was in possession of exploding money. It was programmed to go off when he arrived at his destination and started counting the loot. The kidnapper led the cops right to the hideout. It was an old warehouse. One car brought Father Raaser back to the rectory. Norman told him to go straight to bed. In the morning Norman asked Father Raaser if he heard anything unusual that could hint at who the kidnappers were. After he thought about it Father Raaser said: "Yes. I think I do remember something. He talked about priests learning about following instructions in the seminary. Only a former seminarian would know that."

Norman asked: "What seminary did you attend?"

Father Raaser said: "I attended St. Sebastian's Seminary down on Seminary Row. It is located in the mountains."

Norman asked: "What year were you ordained?"

Father Raaser said; "I was ordained in the year 2005."

Norman asked: "Was there anyone who didn't make it to graduation?"

Father Raaser said: "Yes. His name was Jean Pomeroy. As memory serves me he was an alumnus of this school."

Norman asked: "Was he a disgruntled student?"

Father Raaser said: "I don't think he ever had any love for St. Peter's."

Norman go on the radio and said: "All units report the rectory immediately."

There was a stampede of about 50 plain clothes cops came running into the rectory living room. They all lined up in rows like soldiers. Norman said; "Here are your assignments. Schapiro, John, the rest of squad 1, squad 2, squad 3 and squad 4. Pan out and do another search for Sr. Angelus. The rest of you go to the school and convent. Search every inch of there ground. Any questions?"

Officer Alex said: "Excuse me sir. The school is open today. All those kids will see us."

Norman said: "Then be discreet.. Put on your best face and don't scare the children. DISMISSED!!!"

Norman said: "Officer Alex, report to Sister Angelus' office and show that you are there. Any questions direct them to Sr. Philomena."

Officer Alex said: "Yes sir. It will be done."

They all scattered to the school with Officer Alex in the lead. Sister Philomena got on the intercom and announced that all teachers should keep their doors open. Sister Philomena escorted Officer Alex into the first grade classroom. They all jumped up and said: "Good morning Sister Philomena."

Sr. Philomena said: "Good morning children. This is Officer Alex. He is looking for Sister Angelus. We believe she might be hiding in the school somewhere. You will see a lot of strangers hanging around the school today. They have been inspected by me and I have spoken to their boss. Do not be afraid of them. I must ask you not to leave the classroom today. Try not to wander to the bathroom."

Mitzy was a shy little girl who asked a question. She asked: "Did you talk to Sister Angelus this weekend?"

Sister Philomena said: "No Mitzy. The gentlemen are here to help me find her. If it is urgent to use the bathroom just go as quickly as possible and come straight back here. Please keep the door open today."

She told Officer Alex that Mitzy wets her pants a lot. She did have sympathy for a child with that kind of problem.

CHAPTER 10

Meanwhile back at the rectory they all went to the church. They decided to walk from the outside and not take the back stairs. They entered the church and went straight to the altar rail.

Norman said: "Line up against the altar rail." They did and Norman said: "John, Robert, you are with me. Father Raaser, sit in the first pew and don't move a muscle. He did and did not move the whole day.

Then he said: "Squads 3,4 search the downstairs and every nook and cranny in this place. Robert will show you. Be back here in 3 minutes. If you see a hallway, walk down it. If you see a closet, open it and empty it. Shake out whatever is hanging. Return everything the way you found it. DISMISSED!!!" Everybody scattered. In 3 minutes flat Robert reappeared at the altar in front of Norman. They all had the walkie talkies on. They were told to communicate through them.

Norman said: "The rest of you rework the crime scene from two years ago. Search every nook and cranny up here. They scattered to all the confessionals, the Baptismal Font, the rafters on the ceiling. All 3 of them stayed together. Father Raaser kept turning around and watching the developments. He took notice of their progress. They got to the third confessional when they heard on the walkie talkie that they found her alive. They were downstairs in the basement sacristy. She was hiding in the dark with duck tape around her mouth. She was also tied up with rope around her ankles and wrists. She wasn't able to scream or move. They heard the herd of elephants running into the church. Robert stayed behind to escort the rest of the squad downstairs. Sister Philomena led the charge. She stopped in the office momentarily to announce that Sister Angelus has been found alive. The whole school erupted in applause and screaming YEAH!!! She left instructions to continue on with lesson plans as scheduled. The lockdown was canceled. The teachers did as they were told. They were starting to realize that she was okay and friendly if they did as they were told. They also put on their best face to make Sister Angelus look good. Sister Angelus was gently laid down on the floor. They didn't have an evidence bag big enough for the chair she was sitting on. Norman told Officer Alex to remove the chair to the trunk of the car. It was to be used as evidence in the trial. First she had to endure the indignity of having her picture taken from several angles. Norman and Robert spoke soothing words to her. Her breathing was coming in better as she calmed down. Then came the difficult job of pulling the duct tape off her mouth. Norman had the bright idea to rip it off. When he did she let out a scream. Her mouth was raw and she had to take a few deep breaths. They had to take the ropes off without cutting them. That was tricky.

Norman said: "Officer Alex, call for an ambulance and a stretcher. She has to have a medical exam. Stand outside and direct them down here. You and John and Robert will escort her and stay with her the rest of the day. Give her a ride home tonight. Tomorrow morning we can start putting together the official report.

Robert said: "Excuse me sir. They might keep her overnight for observation at least."

Norman said: "If they do that then one of you will stand guard outside her hospital room all night. Figure out whom will do that. Be down in the precinct tomorrow morning at 9:00 a.m. Good night."

CHAPTER 11

The paramedics arrived and Officer Alex showed them through. The paramedics gloved up and did her blood pressure and pulse chick. She was put in a cervical collar just in case of spinal injuries. She was very cooperative throughout the procedure.

Norman said: "Tomorrow Robert will interview you about your kidnapping ordeal. For now he and John They will escort you to the hospital and then drive you back to the convent."

Sister Angelus smiled and said: "Thank you Norman. I will do all that I can to assist you." Everybody dispensed at this point and went their separate ways.

At the hospital they were met by a Dr. David Tanner. He came into room 3 and introduced himself. By the time he got there she was already in a hospital gown waiting to be seen. Robert and John left the room until the nurse came and got them. They didn't want to see a nun in a state of undress. Sister Angelus knew they were professional, but still had hormones running through them.

The nurse said: "We will do a medical exam and rape kit as part of it. Since you are a victim of a crime this is standard procedure. I will stay with you during the exam and explain everything that is being done before he does it. You can stop him at any time."

Sister Angelus said: "May I have these two cops in here with me?"

The nurse said: "Certainly sister." She left and Robert and John entered the room.

John asked: "How are you feeling sister?"

Sister Angelus said: "I am hungry, thirsty tired and generally exhausted, but otherwise I am still alive. I do have one question though. From a legal standpoint do I have a right to refuse a rape exam?"

Robert fielded that one and said: "Yes sister. You do have that right. There is a pill we give you to prevent pregnancy."

Sister Angelus said: "Dr. Tanner, I am 100% certain that I was not touched in that fashion. I would like to forgo the rape exam, but I am willing to take the pill to prevent pregnancy."

Dr. Tanner said: "Of course sister. But I must caution you that the longer you wait the less likely we will find evidence of a crime."

Sister Angelus said: "Do the blood test for STD detection."

John said: "Wait sister. I have a better idea. Why don't you get the doctor to put you to sleep? That way he can do his job."

Dr. Tanner said: "Thank you John. Now you can get your evidence."

Detective Schapiro and John went to the convent and announced that Sister Angelus will be spending the night in the hospital. In the morning the two detectives arrived at the hospital to pick up Sister Angelus. Detective Schapiro brought a spare dress and panties for Sister Angelus to wear home. She was driven to the convent. Sister Philomena was there to greet her and bring her some tea and toast.

Detective Schapiro said: "Sister Angelus, we need to go over what happened as soon as possible."

Sister Philomena said: "Tomorrow I will bring her down to the precinct and you can have her all day."

Detective Schapiro said: "Norman will come to pick you up at 8:30 a.m."

Sister Philomena said: "Roger and out. Good night Schapiro."

Robert called the precinct and told Norman of the latest developments. He and John reported to the precinct right away for a day of work.

At the meeting the next day Norman told Robert and John that he secretly was afraid of Sister Philomena. He told them he is their boss, but don't cross that woman.

CHAPTER 12

The next morning Sister Angelus woke up at 6:00 and had breakfast. It was a light one of toast and coffee. She didn't have much of an appetite. Sr. Philomena opened the school building. She stayed in the school and played substitute principal for the last day. Norman drove up at 8:00 a.m. right on time. John jumped out and ran up and rang the doorbell. He held her by the hand and kept looking around like a nervous rabbit. She secretly enjoyed the extra attention and let herself be led away to the car. She was put into the back seat and Norman told John to sit in the front seat with him. He jumped out and put on the seatbelt of Sister Angelus and locked her door. Norman screamed out to stop slamming the door. Norman looked back at Sister Angelus and found her grinning at him. Norman asked: "Good morning Sister Angelus. How are you today?"

Sister Angelus said: "Fine thank you."

Norman asked: "Did you sleep will last night?"

Sister Angelus said: "Yes sir. I slept like a baby. In the hospital I was given anesthesia, so I guess I was still groggy from that."

Norman said: "Glad to hear it sister. Are you ready for this?"

Sister Angelus said: "Yes sir. I am ready to cooperate fully. I want to do everything I can to get these people."

Norman started the car and drove off.

CHAPTER 13

They arrived at the precinct about 45 minutes later. All three of them were led to Robert Schapiro's office. He led them to what is known as the inquisition room. It was a bland room with a one way mirror. Norman and John stood on the other side and witnessed the questioning from the other side. Robert appeared with a plate of cookies and 2 cups of tea.

Robert asked: "So. How did you sleep last night?"

Sister Angelus said: "Fine thank you. They gave me anesthesia in the hospital. I think I was still groggy from that."

Robert said: "That takes maybe a week to go out of your system. How long it takes depends on how much you were given. The best thing you can do is work through it. Try not to nap during the day. The best thing you can do is to get back to work as soon as possible. Make sure you always have an escort. You will bee the boogie man behind every bush and closed door. Try not to jump out of your skin every time somebody looks at you or bumps into you. Now tell me. Let's revisit everything that happened to you last Friday morning. The day of the kidnapping."

Sister Angelus said: "It really started the Friday before. I was sitting in my office when Sister Philomena appeared unexpectedly. She came just in time because my first grade teacher has to leave because of breast cancer. She agreed to stay and be the substitute. This way I didn't have to pay a high salary or health insurance for a stranger I probably will only see a few months. She really wanted a home cooked meal, so we all ended up at your house on Sunday."

Robert asked: "What were you doing when Sister Philomena showed up?"

Sister Angelus said: "I was planning the week's events and the assembly for Friday. It was Halloween and I wanted to show the kids how to stay safe. I didn't want to sound preachy and tell them don't do this that and the other."

Robert asked: "When did Sister Philomena start working here?"

Sister Angelus said: "She got a very warm reception from everybody. The students, parents, and other teachers seem to take to her."

Robert asked: "Have you had any negative responses at all?"

Sister Angelus said: "No. Not even a cross eyed look."

Robert asked: "Are you in agreement with her about her teaching methods?"

Sister Angelus said: "I have not seen her teaching methods yet. I am not going to judge her. She is also the mother superior provincial of the order."

Robert said: "Good God Sister I have been speaking to the mother superior this whole time?" He spit his tea out and almost threw the cup across the room.

Sister Angelus said: "Relax Robert. She isn't the Pope."

Robert asked: "Did they feed you at all?"

Sister Angelus said: "One person gave me soup. He tied a bib around my neck so I don't spill it on my dress. He also gave me a glass of water so I don't dehydrate. He was rather nice to me."

Robert asked: "Did these people seem familiar to you at all?"

Sister Angelus said: "Maybe. I am still trying to figure that out."

Robert asked: "How many people were there?"

Sister Angelus said: "There were two people taking care of me, but I heard two more voices. I did not actually see them."

Robert asked: "When did you first realize you were in trouble?"

Sister Angelus said; "As soon as it happened. At first I thought it was the parents playing a joke on me."

Robert asked: "Where did they take you when they took you?"

Sister Angelus said: "They put me in the closet right where you found me. When I first opened my eyes I didn't realize I was in a church or that I was in St. Peter's either. It was an empty closet. I didn't realize what was supposed to be there. It was just empty."

Robert asked: Did the voices sound familiar at all?"

Sister Angelus said: "No. I was trying to place them, but nothing rings any bells."

Norman walked in and interrupted the interview. John walked in and took a seat. Robert walked out and Norman said: "We have a lead. Drive Sister Angelus back to the school and return to the station."

Robert did as he was told.

CHAPTER 14

Sister Philomena saw Sister Angelus came out of the cop car and she ran to the door to greet her. They hugged each other and came back to the office. Sister Philomena announced on the intercom to report to the gym immediately. Within 10 minutes everybody was assembled in the gym. There was no time to assemble the chairs. Everybody just stood in a row where they would normally sit.

Sister Philomena said: "I apologize to the teachers for interrupting your day and lesson plans. I have a surprise for you. Please come out now."

At that point Sister Angelus appeared on the stage. The whole gym erupted into screaming and applause.

Sister Angelus said: "I am really happy to be back. Everybody do one extra page of homework tonight to make up for the time you are not in class."

The children all groaned and did this gladly just to have Sister Angelus back. It was the end of the school day, so the children returned to the classrooms for dismissal. Sister Philomena and Sister Angelus spent time in the office catching up on the latest news of the school. Sister Philomena was glad to return to the classroom to teach the first grade. They walked back to the convent and got to work on their school stuff. Sister Angelus was glad to be back in the office chair. John returned to the precinct after he dropped off the two nuns at the convent.

CHAPTER 15

Robert asked: "Norman, why did you stop the interview like that?"

Norman said: "We caught one perpetrator. Officer Alex will come back with the perpetrator. We are waiting now for his arrival."

Robert said: "Impressive. How did we do that?"

Norman said: "That will become clear when the story comes out."

Officer Alex returned with the kidnapper in handcuffs. He was taken to the inquisition room and Robert took care of the questioning.

Robert asked: "What is your name?"

Jean said: "My name is Jean Pomeroy."

Robert asked: "How many people were involved in this caper?"

Jean said: "There was me and my wife and my neighbors."

Robert asked: "How did they fit in to this caper?"

Jean said: "My wife and neighbors showed up in a bertha. My neighbor was also dressed all in black. We all had Uzis, but they were unloaded."

Robert asked: "Was this because of the children that they were unloaded?"

Jean said: "Yes. We had no beef with the children. It was Father Raaser we were after. Accidents can happen."

Robert said: "You successfully frightened the bejesus out of the children. You are under arrest for kidnapping. Stand up and put your hands behind your back. You have a right to remain silent. You have a right to an attorney. If you cannot afford one one will be appointed to you. Do you understand these rights as I have explained them to you?"

Jean said: "Yes I do."

Robert said: "You will now be taken down to a holding cell to await arraignment. Arraignment will take place in the morning. You will be given a cell and dinner tonight. You will stay in your cell until you are called upon. If you cooperate fully the judge might just go easy on you. Where are your wife and neighbors?"

Jean said: "I haven't seen them since I was taken away from my home earlier today."

Robert asked: "Before we depart do you have any questions for me?"

Jean said: "Yes I do. What will happen at arraignment?"

Robert said: "You will be read a list of your charges. They you will plead guilty or not guilty."

Jean asked: "Will I have a lawyer then?"

Robert said: "Yes. Your lawyer will do all the talking for you. You will meet with him before hand to get your story straight."

Jean said: "Okay. Got it."

Jean was taken to a holding cell at that point. He didn't make any trouble or noise. The guards treated him nicely because of his cooperation.

CHAPTER 16

The next day Jean was taken to court just as he was told it would happen. The judge said: "Jean, you are being charged with the kidnapping of a nun. How do you plead?"

Jean's lawyer said: "Jean pleads guilty your honor."

The judge said: "Well. This is a surprise. A defendant pleading guilty makes my job much easier. You are being held over for trail without bond or bail."

Jeans lawyer said: "Your honor, my client is clearly not a flight risk. He has no money or passport. We respectfully request that you release my client ROR."

The judge said: "Request denied. Remove the defendant to the tombs. Next case."

Jean's wife Margie was the next person to go before the judge. Margie received the same fate as

Jean. Held over for trial. The neighbors happen to have skipped town. Margie was also charged with kidnapping. She was confident that she would get off. She suffered the same fate as her husband. The judge allowed Margie to stay in the same cell as her husband Jean. She made a direct order not to have sexual contact with each other. She agreed to that right away. She was taken downstairs to the tombs and processed. She had her picture taken, fingerprints taken, and DNA taken. The strip search was the worst part of it. She never had anybody look up her heiney hole before. Then she was taken to her husband's cell for a hot meal. They were given hot coffee on the assumption they wouldn't throw it at each other.

CHAPTER 17

J ury selection started and ended the next day. They were to be tried together to save the court time and money. They picked 12 jurors with 2 alternates. One person got out of it because she was a nun. The judge's name was Joe Murphy. The jurors broke for lunch and were told to come back for instructions. After lunch everybody returned right on time.

Judge Joe said: "Good afternoon everyone. Thank you for being punctual. This trial will start tomorrow morning at 9:00 a.m. Please be punctual.. This trial will not run too long. We will not be sequestering you. We will not be letting you out too late. I know you have families. Please assemble right here. Your name tags will be sent downstairs and you will be marked present. Two people are missing in this case. After they are found they will be tried by a separate jury. There is an APB out and a warrant for their arrest. You will not consider their involvement in your deliberations. You will only consider the facts for these two defendants. This is a nonviolent case. You will not hear ridiculous questions about their childhood grades in school. We are now adjourned until tomorrow morning 9:00 a.m. Good day everyone."

The bailiff yelled: "ALL RISE!!!"

Everybody rose and left the courtroom.

CHAPTER 18

Day 1 of the trial started at 9:00. Everybody was on time, which put the judge in a good mood to start the day.

The judge said: "Good morning everyone. Thank you for being on time. This trial will be conducted with the utmost decorum and respect. We will not have interruptions every 5 minutes. The lawyers are free to disagree with each other, but they will talk about it in my chambers, not here. With that being said does anyone have any questions?"

Juror number 5 said: "Excuse me sir. Does the jury have a right to question the witnesses?"

Judge Murphy said: "No sir. Only lawyers have a right to ask questions. That only happens in Florida. You are only to consider the evidence in your court case. It is up to the lawyers to tell you what they want to tell you."

Juror number 5 said: "Thank you sir."

Judge Murphy said: "With that I turn it over to the lawyers for opening statements.

The prosecuting attorney's name was Paul Flannery. Paul got up and said: "Ladies and gentlemen of the jury. My name is Paul Flannery. My job is to convince you that these two people are guilty of the crime of extortion and kidnapping in the first degree. Thank you."

The defense attorney's name was Peter O'Grady. Peter got up and said: "Ladies and gentlemen of the jury. It is no secret that my clients did this heinous act. The problem is that nobody saw them do it. All they have is circumstantial evidence. Without a cooperating witness there is no crime. Thank you."

CHAPTER 19

Judge Joe said: "Paul, call your first witness please."

Paul got up and said: "I call Sr. Angelus to the stand."

As sister Angelus approached the stand she was sworn in as the witness.

Paul said: "Sr. Angelus. Please tell us how you got involved in this case."

Sister Angelus said: "I was the victim in this case. I was the one who was kidnapped."

Paul asked: "How are you related to Sr. Philomena?"

Sister Angelus said: "Sr. Philomena is my mother superior. She is in charge of the whole order."

Paul asked: "What was Sister Philomena doing at your school?"

Sister Angelus said: "She was checking up on me to see what kind of work I do. She comes around about once every five years. She is responsible for bringing me any help I may need."

Paul asked: "How did she get to Las Vegas?"

Sister Angelus said: "She flew in an airplane."

Paul asked: "Who paid for her ticket?"

Sister Angelus said: "She wears the old time habit. There are still good Catholics out there who will go out of their way to help a nun. This time it was somebody at the airport. He brought her ticket and she laughed all the way over here."

Paul asked: "How did she find you once she got off the plane?"

Sister. Angelus said: "When she got off the plane she found a group of cops standing around in a circle. She saw their badges and guns, so she asked them for directions. They gave her a ride to the school. It turns out that she found a group of detective friends of mine."

Peter asked: "Excuse me sir. May I ask for a meeting with you?"

The judge said: "Okay. We will adjourn until tomorrow morning. We will adjourn to my chambers.'

CHAPTER 20

In chambers the judge said: "What seems to be the problem Paul?"

Paul said: "I am upset about this line of questioning. Sr. Angelus was the victim. Why would you spend so much time talking about somebody else? Sr. Philomena's travels do not bear any resemblance to the kidnapping of Sr. Angelus."

The judge said: "Peter, how do you respond to these objections?"

Peter said: "I am merely putting her at ease. Testifying before a jury is probably something she has never done before."

Paul said: "As a matter of fact she has testified before. She seems perfectly relaxed to me."

The judge asked: "How do you know this Peter?"

Peter said: "I have my sources I prefer not to reveal."

The judge said: "Very well. But from now on keep your questions directed only to Sr Angelus. Leave Sr. Philomena out of it. She can testify for herself. Happy now Paul?"

Paul said: "Yes sir. Thank you sir."

The judge said: "We are done for the day. Go home and show your wives your ugly mugs. Get reacquainted with them. Come back to court prepared tomorrow."

Nobody knew this but Paul pulled this as a scam to get home. He wasn't in the mood to be at work that day. If anybody knew that he would get fired for sure. That is why he objected to nothing. Secretly he really didn't care where Peter was going with this. He vowed to never do that again. He was suffering from burnout of his job. He had to plan the perfect time for this. Instead of going home he went to the mall for lunch. He almost choked on his food when he saw the judge pass him.

The judge said: "Oh! Good afternoon Paul. I took advantage of the afternoon off. I guess you did the same thing."

Paul said: "Yes sir. I see a lot of people in the mall. I thought maybe I would look for a new suit while I am here. Doesn't anybody work anymore?"

The judge said: "Most of these people are tourists. Las Vegas is a very hot city, so most people work at night. The night air is much cooler and easier to take. Did you find a new suit?"

Paul said: "I haven't found the right store yet. I probably need to go to the Big and Tall store for men."

The judge said: "My next stop is the Petco next door. I have a cat and I need to buy the food and litter. See you tomorrow."

With that they parted company. Paul weaseled his way out of that one.

CHAPTER 21

Day two of the trail started at 9:00 right on time.

The judge entered and the bailiff yelled "ALL RISE!!!" Everybody rose and waited for the judge to be seated.

The judge said: "Good morning everyone. Thank you for being punctual. Sr. Angelus, please return to the stand. Remember you are still under oath."

Sister Angelus took her seat in the witness box.

Peter said: "I have no more questions your honor."

The judge said: "Paul, do you have any questions for this witness?"

Paul said: "Yes sir. Now Sister Angelus, how did these people get into the school?"

Sister Angelus said: "I assume they came in the front door. Any other ideas might come from the cops."

Paul asked: "Do you always leave the front door open with no guards?"

Sister Angelus said: "We never had a problem with anybody. In the beginning of the year the parents are instructed to come straight to the office. All teaches are trained to question strangers wandering around the halls."

Paul asked: "How did the defendants know where to find you? Are you not normally in the office?"

Sister Angelus said: "We have never figured that out. According to the school secretary nobody came to this office."

Paul asked: "Did you tell the children you will be in the gym on that day ahead of time?"

Sister Angelus said: "No. These surprise assemblies come up spontaneously."

Paul asked: "Do you think it was an inside job?"

Sister Angelus said: "I haven't figured that you yet."

Paul asked: "When did you first realize you were taken to St. Peter's church?"

Sister Angelus said: "When Robert threw open the door and I saw all the cops staring at me. He had to tell me where I was."

Paul said: "No more questions your honor."

The judge said: "You may step down Sister Angelus. Peter, call your next witness please."

CHAPTER 22

The judge said: "Peter, call your next witness please."

Peter said: " I call Robert Schapiro to the stand."

As Robert approached the stand he was sworn in as the next witness. He took his seat in the witness box.

Peter asked: "When were you called into this case?"

Robert said: "On the day of the kidnapping I received a phone call and was told of the situation. I went to the school and then we all gathered in the church to come up with a plan."

Peter asked: "How long was it before you found her?"

Robert said: "I think it was the next day. When I get involved in a case I lose all track of time. We gathered at the altar rail and came up with a plan."

Peter asked: "Who called you?"

Robert said: "It was our friend Ronald. His daughter is a student there in the first grade. She panicked and called her father to call me."

Peter asked: "What is her name?"

Robert said: "Her name is Arlene. Sister Philomena said she was sitting in the front row. Sister Philomena gave her permission to use her cell phone. Sister Philomena already knew Ronald and Arlene. She didn't want to abuse the privilege, so she made it short. Sister Philomena took the phone and filled him in."

Peter asked: "How did you come about fingering the defendant for the crime?"

Robert said: "It was Father Raaser who put it together. There is a plague on the wall of the church with all the priests names and dates they served the parish. The archbishop himself called each person and everybody was accounted for. That eliminated a lot of names. Most of them offered their assistance to resolve the situation. The archbishop kindly turned them down because we didn't need too many people getting in the way.

Peter asked: "Who came up with the ransom money?"

Robert said: "The archdiocese came up with the money. The archbishop was the liason with the money."

Peter asked: "When were you first contacted about the ransom?"

Robert said: "I don't remember. I lose track of time whenever I get involved in a case."

Peter asked: "Would you please answer my question now? How did you find the defendant?"

Robert said: "Oh sorry. The defendant was a roommate of Father Raaser's in the seminary. He didn't make it to ordination. He quit before he was finished. He was a graduate of St. Peter's school. Sister Angelus was his first grade teacher. He knew she was still a beloved member of St. Peter's parish."

Paul said: "Objection your honor. Robert is in no position to determine what my client thinks or thought."

Robert said: "Actually he admitted it in his interview after his arrest."

The judge said: "Overruled. The jury will remember the witness' remarks and accept them into the record."

Peter said: "No more questions your honor."

The judge said: "Paul, do you have any questions for this witness?"

Paul said: "Yes sir. Robert, what did Father Raaser do when you looked for Sister Angelus?"

Robert said: "Norman told him to sit in the first pew and not to move. He stayed there all day. I noticed him turning around watching us."

Paul asked: "Was this the first incident at the church?"

Robert said; "No. We repeated what wed did a few years ago. Another team searched the downstairs and there she was in the closet. We all trampled down the stairs. We sounded like a herd of elephants running."

Paul asked: "Did you use Commissioner the horse in this investigation?"

Robert said: "No. We were assuming she was in one of the buildings near by. Probably on church property. Commissioner is not like a tracking dog. I cannot give him a piece of her dress to sniff and have him find her. I don't think Commissioners knows about the basement."

Paul asked: "Did you use Daisy your Beagle dog?"

Robert said: "Yes. I drove home and brought him to the church. She was with me the whole day. If we went back to a place we already searched Daisy would send me a signal that we were already there."

Paul asked: "Was it your dog that found her?"

Robert said: "No sir. It was the cop. Daisy and I were upstairs when the call came in. When she heard it she ran toward the sacristy. I told her to stay at the top of the stairs because I didn't want her to get stepped on. It was a rather small space down in there. She always obeys my commands. She stood there and barked at everybody."

Paul said: "No more questions your honor."

The judge said: "You may step down Robert."

Robert stepped down and returned to his seat.

The judge said: "We will break for lunch now. Everybody be back here in one hour for the afternoon session."

When everybody returned the judge said: "Peter, you may call your next witness please."

Peter said: "I call Archbishop McCloskey to the stand."

As Archbishop McCloskey approached he was sworn in as the next witness. He was so nervous he tripped on the step going up to his seat.

The judge said: "Relax Archbishop. Is this your first time on the witness stand?

Archbishop McCloskey said: "Yes sir. I have never done this before." He suffered extreme dry mouth, so his voice was croaky and very hoarse.

The judge asked: "Would you like a glass of water?"

Archbishop said: "Thank you sir."

Peter said: "Just try and relax and tell only the truth. don't worry about the outcome. Your only role here is to answer the questions we ask you."

The judge said: "That's right Archbishop. Peter, remember who you are talking to. You and Paul will speak to him with the respect and dignity as anyone else. No pressure."

Peter asked: "How did you get involved in this case?"

Archbishop McCloskey said: "I was the one who got the money together for the ransom. I was told of the situation by Father Raaser. My role was to read all the names on the plague and call every one of the priests who appeared on that board. They were the names of all the former priests. All of their whereabouts were verified and I was satisfied that they were preoccupied with other projects for the time in question. Most of them offered their services to help out any way they can. I gently turned them down because if there were too many people the work would get scrambled and confused. They all promised to pray for her safe return. Sure enough they did because she did turn up that afternoon. I called all of them and reported that she is safe and in the hospital."

Peter asked: "Since the defendant did not make it to ordination where did his name come from? How did you happen to zero in on him specifically?"

Archbishop McCloskey said: "It was Father Raaser who came up with his name. His voice came over the phone and the cops figured out where he was calling from. From there it was just a matter of deduction."

Peter said: "No more questions your honor."

The judge said: "Paul, do you have any questions for this witness?"

Paul said: "No more questions your honor."

The judge said: "Very well. We will break for the day. Everybody return here tomorrow morning at 9:00 a.m. for the morning session."

With that everybody rose and left the courtroom.

CHAPTER 23

Outside court Robert's phone rang. It was Norman.

Norman asked; "Robert, is John with you?"

Robert said: "Yes sir. He is in the bathroom."

Norman said: "I need you two back at the station house right away. Come to your office and we will adjourn to an interrogation room."

Robert said: "Right away sir."

John approached and was directed to the car. John asked: "What does Norman want?"

Robert said: "He didn't say. He just said to come to my office and he will fill us in. Look in that shopping bag in the back seat. There are two water bottles in there. Bring them to the front and open mine for me. I can't because I am driving." He did as he was told and John practically drank the whole bottle in one slug.

Robert said: "Good heavens John. No wonder you are always in the bathroom. I will not take it away from you."

After Robert parked the car he brought out the water, belched loudly, and went up to his office. From there they went to the interrogation room and was surprised to see Mary sitting there drinking a cup of coffee. They each greeted her pleasantly and exchanged pleasantries with each other.

John asked: "Has Norman been entertaining you?"

Mary said: "Oh yes. He has been a most gracious host. We were just sitting here chewing the fat and talking. By the way. This coffee taste like shoe polish. We really need your wife to come in and make a pot. Let's get down to the real season I came here. Norman tells me you are quite the mystery solver. We have a mystery going on in my jail. We have had 5 deaths of inmates in my jail. The autopsy shows nothing out of the ordinary. My superiors are starting to take notice."

John asked: "Were these deaths of the general population?"

Mary said: "No. These were isolation unit people."

John asked: "Did they finish their last meal?"

Mary said: "Yes. There was nothing left on their plate."

John asked: "Were these deaths occurring in a pattern?"

Mary asked: "What do you mean by that?"

John said: "I mean was it once a week or once every two weeks or randomly timed?"

Mary said; "I think it was once a week."

John said: "That is obvious. It was probably somebody spiking the food with anti freeze. It is tasteless and probably mixed in with soup. I don't know how they hid the color green of the liquid."

Mary said: "Thank you John. I will have the pathologist check their blood for that."

Norman said: "I told you he can figure it out."

John said; "Once more thing Mary. You might need to exhume the bodies. You will need a court order and the permission of the families for that."

Robert said: "That was good thinking John. I knew we could count on you."

A week later Mary called and said; it was anti freeze in the food. It made sense because only certain prisoners died. Not the rest of them.

John said: "What you have to do is to investigate the road the food traveled. I would start with the cooks in the kitchen. Then move on to the guards delivering the food. Start strip searching even the guards to make sure they are not carrying it in. Just remember the anti freeze is not walking in there on its own power. Obviously somebody is carrying it in. Did these prisoners live through the night?"

Mary said: "We don't know. As near as we can tell it happened sometime in the night."

John asked: "Were these troublemakers or hardened criminals?"

Mary said: "No. These were in here for armed robbery. They weren't troublemakers at all."

John asked: Did these prisoners take the boot camp program?"

Mary said: "Yes. They all did. They all passed with flying colors."

John said: "I would also investigate the drill sergeant in order to eliminate him. Find out if he had a vendetta against them."

Mary said: "I will do all that. Thanks John. I knew I could count on you."

When Mary left Robert said: "That was good thinking John. You actually gave her a stepping point to start with."

CHAPTER 24

Day three of the trial started at 9:00 right on time. The bailiff yelled: "ALL RISE!!!"

Everybody rose and the judge entered the room. He said good morning to the jury. Then he said: "Peter, call your first witness please."

Peter said: "I call Father Raaser to the stand." As Father Raaser approached he was sworn in as the next witness.

Peter asked: "Father Raaser, how did you get involved in this case?"

Father Raaser said: "This event happened in my parish. Sr. Angelus is a beloved member of our team."

Peter asked: "How do you know the detectives?"

Father Raaser said; "They are all parishioners of mine. They go to Mass whenever possible."

Peter asked: "Do they ever go to confession in your parish?"

Father Raaser said: "We only do the confessions in the old fashioned confessional. It is a darkened box behind the screen. Even if they did I wouldn't know it was them. Nobody knows this but I installed a box in the confessor's side. This box scrambled the voice so I don't recognize who it is. Sometimes I have to stop myself from giggling and laughing at the sound."

The judge said: "Be very careful Peter. You know you are not allowed to ask a priest about a confessions. That would be breaking the Church's rules of confidentiality. Move on Peter."

Peter asked; "How did you happen to zero in on the defendant?"

Father Raaser said: "At the time we talked it over Robert asked me if anybody had a vendetta against me. I remembered my old roommate in the seminary. He wasn't a happy man with Sister Angelus. For some reason he didn't like her. I think it was me he was after. Taking away from me the one thing that is most important to me. I think it was another teacher he had that I always defended. She was a child of God no matter what her transgressions are or were."

Peter asked: "Is this nun still alive?"

Father Raaser said: "I don't know. When I came back to Saint Peter's as a priest nobody seemed to know who she was."

Peter asked: "Did you ask the archbishop or the cardinal about her?"

Father Raaser said: "I am not really interested. I just pray that she found peace with herself. He also didn't agree with the church's teachings about certain subjects."

Peter said: "No more questions your honor."

The judge said: "Paul, do you have any questions for this witness?"

Paul said: "Yes your honor. Father Raaser, how is your parish doing financially?"

Father Raaser said: "We pay our bills comfortably. I am not alone in my parish running everything. I get a lot of help from 2 associates. Part of my job is to mold one priest at a time into something resembling a priest. My parish is usually their first assignment. I have been getting at least one priest from each ordination class for twenty years now. We pay our bills because a lot of people give us chips from the casino. Everybody in all the casinos know me and when I am coming in the front door. I have heard the chatter on the walkie talkies from the security. They say: St. Peters coming in the front door." I laugh at that. I just pretended not to hear, but I was laughing all the way over to the redemption center. A lot of our parishioners are these people. We smile and joke with each other."

Paul asked: "Father Raaser, did you ever talk to the defendant?"

Father Raaser said: "No. I heard him on the speaker phone. Robert told me not to make a sound. Since I went to the seminary with him he would recognize me. I never actually saw him though. There was a black car near by with dark tinted windows. I heard from somebody about obedience. Only a seminarian would know about that. He used a few Latin phrases. That is when I knew for sure who was behind this caper."

Paul asked: "Did you drop the money off at the park?"

Father Raaser said: "Yes. In the second lamp post at a certain place."

Paul asked: "Did Sister Angelus talk to you when you found her?"

Father Raaser said: "No. I hung back and let the cops do their job. I was satisfied when I saw she was breathing. After paramedics took over and the cops took their pictures I hung up all the chausibles and straightened out everything. Norman promised to keep me informed of her condition."

Paul asked: "Have you ever testified in a courtroom before?"

Father Raaser said: "Yes. Several times. I know all about telling the truth."

Paul asked: "Did anybody coach you in doing this?"

Father Raaser said: "Robert reminded me about the rules of courtroom edicut. Make sure my suit is clean and things like that. He told me to make sure I shave and wash my hair. He said no cursing our interrupting is allowed. I didn't need too much coaching. It has been several years since my last time testifying."

Paul said: "No more questions your honor."

The judge said: "You may step down Father. We will dismiss you for the day. Everybody return here tomorrow morning at 9:00 a.m. Have a nice evening."

The bailiff yelled: ALL RISE!!!"

With that everybody rose and left the courtroom

CHAPTER 25

Day four of the trial started at 9:00 exactly. As the judge entered the bailiff yelled : "ALL RISE!!!" Everybody rose and the judge entered.

The judge said: "Good morning ladies and gentlemen. Peter, call your first witness please."

Peter said: "I call Jean the defendant to the stand."

As Jean approached the stand he was sworn in as the witness.

Peter asked: "Were you involved in the kidnapping of Sr. Angelus?"

Jean said: "Yes sir. I did it with a little help from my neighbors."

Peter asked: "What role did your neighbors play in this caper?"

Jean said: "They stood on the two sides with machine guns pointed at the children."

Peter asked: "Were the guns loaded?"

Jean said: "No. But nobody knew that though. We had no intention of harming the children."

Peter asked: "Did you hold the kids hostage?"

Jean said: "No. We just grabbed Sr. Angelus and high tailed it out of there. The kids thought it was a Halloween trick about safety. That is what the lecture was about."

Peter asked: "Who mucked up your plans?"

Jean said: "That wicked Sister Philomena did when she hot mouthed my neighbor. She almost cracked her knuckles with the ruler if she had one."

Peter asked: "Why did you do this heinous act?"

Jean said: "I was really after the Church's money. I knew the Cardinal would spend the money in order to keep a nun safe. They have to pressure the order after all."

Peter asked: "Where was your wife during this event?"

Jean said: "She was on the other side of the gym. She pointed the machine gun at the kids, but when Sr. Philomena hot mouthed my neighbor she also ran away out the side door."

Peter asked: "Why didn't you kidnap the Cardinal instead?"

Jean said: "If I did that half the city of Las Vegas would be looking for him. Since I decided to kidnap a nun the children were powerless to get involved."

Peter asked: "How did you know where to find Sister Angelus?"

Jean said: "My neighbor's kids told us where they will be. They said there was an assembly for Halloween. That is when I hatched this plan."

Peter asked: "Are you a former student of Sister Angelus?"

Jean said: "No. But I was tortured by a nun who dressed like Sister Angelus."

Peter said: " No more questions your honor."

The judge said: " Paul, do you have any questions for this witness?"

Paul said: "Yes sir. Now Jean, have you ever had psychiatric help for your problems?"

Jean said: "No. Psychiatry is a farce. I can talk to my own family for free. Talking to a psychiatrist doesn't change the way the nuns treated me. I can also talk to any stranger on the street for free. It won't cost me the cost of health insurance."

Paul asked: "Did you intend to injure Sister Angelus?"

Jean said: "No. Injury to her was never an option. All we did was lock her in a closet for a few days."

Paul asked: "Did you feed her or give her water?"

Jean said: "We fed her once a day. We gave her one glass of water a day."

Paul asked: "Was she dehydrated when she was found?"

Jean said: "I don't know. But I pinched her and her skin went back down on her hand."

Paul said: "No more questions your honor."

The judge said: "You may step down Jean. After lunch we will start with closing arguments. Everybody return here in one hour."

Peter interrupted and said: "Excuse me your honor. May we call one more witness?"

The judge said: "Who is it Peter?"

Peter said: "It is the doctor she saw in the hospital. We just now got word that he is available to testify. Being a doctor his schedule is unpredictable."

The judge said: "Very well. But make it a quick testimony. We really want to get through the closing arguments today. Paul, are there any objections to this sudden appearance of the witness?"

Paul said: "No objections your honor."

The judge said: "We will break for lunch now. Everybody be back here in one hour."

Everybody returned and the judge said: "Peter, call your next witness please."

Peter said: "I call Dr. David Tanner to the stand."

Dr. Tanner approached the stand and was sworn in as the next and final witness.

Peter asked: "Dr. Tanner, how did you get involved in this case?"

Dr. Tanner said: "I was the doctor at the emergency room who examined Sister Angelus."

Peter asked: "What kind of patient was Sister Angelus?"

Dr. Tanner said: "She was very cooperative. The only thing she objected to was the rape kit. I agreed to skip that part on the assumption she would take the morning after pill. She assured me that the kidnappers didn't touch her in that way. I left it at that."

Peter asked: "Did you see her in a state of undress?"

Dr. Tanner said: "No. Only the female nurses saw her and helped her into the hospital gown. Robert, John, and I waited outside to give her some privacy. She looks nothing different than any other female victim. She is entitled to some dignity."

Peter asked: "Did you ultimately do the rape kit?"

Dr. Tanner said: "Yes. I had to put her under anesthesia to do it. We got no evidence of anything. Robert and John were there when I did it. I also had a female nurse in the room. She was right about not being touched in that way."

Peter asked: "Why is it that you are just now made available for testimony?"

Dr. Tanner said: "I was on vacation in Colorado. It took me time to catch up with my mail. I just read it last night. I called you right away. You told me when to show up in court. Here I am."

Peter asked: "Did Robert and John have to look where a gentleman should only look at his wife?"

Dr. Tanner said: "No. They turned their faces away and they were only at her head. I thought John was going to loose his lunch. Robert also turned rather ashen colored."

I thought we were having 2 fainted patients in the room. They had to sit down. I put John in the bed next to Sister Angelus. When I put her legs down I woke up John and told him he could look. She is then descent. John took out her panties and told me to put them on her. I also put on socks to her feet. Sister Angelus loved the socks. When she woke up she asked if she could keep them." There was giggling from the galley at these comments.

Peter said: "No more questions your honor."

The judge said: "Paul, do you have any questions for this witness?"

Paul said: "No your honor. No questions for this witness."

The judge said: "Very well. We will adjourn until tomorrow morning for closing arguments. Good night everyone."

The bailiff yelled: "ALL RISE!!!" Everybody rose and exited the court room.

CHAPTER 26

Everybody returned in the morning right on time. The judge entered and said: "ALL RISE!!!" He said he knows that is the bailiff's line, but sometimes he gets carried away. He apologized to the bailiff for not letting him do his job. The bailiff smiled and said it's okay.

The judge said: "Peter, you may begin when ready."

Peter said: "thank you your honor. It is no secret that my client did this. You must find him not guilty because he did not cause harm to Sister Angelus. His beef was with the Catholic Church, not Sister Angelus. He did this because the Church rejected him on the basis of his personal beliefs. He was not allowed to think for himself. He had to say and think and do whatever he was told. The Catholic Church took away from him what was sacred. His individuality. What he did was extortion and kidnapping, not murder. He revealed to me he tried to call out for help because of the torture, but nobody answered him. If anything the Catholic Church is responsible for his psychological problems, not him. Thank you your honor."

CHAPTER 27

The judge said: "Paul, you may begin when ready."

Paul said: "Thank you your honor. Ladies and gentlemen of the jury. Jean did this for sure. He should not go to jail however. Instead I ask you to sentence him to volunteer services in a convent.. Just to feed them and drive them around and do their shopping. He obviously has alternate ideas of what the Catholic Church is all about. He obviously doesn't see that nuns aren't all bad. The Catholic Church policies are in place for a reason. He just doesn't understand them. He needs guidance, not punishment. Let's come together and teach this misguided Christian. Thank you."

The jury took just 20 minutes to come back with a guilty verdict. They spent 18 minutes deciding on a punishment for him. Some wanted him in jail, while others wanted him to do volunteer work.

They finally decided to do the road of volunteer work. They sent a note to the judge stating that they reached a verdict. They all gathered back in the court room. The judge said: "Has the jury reached a verdict?"

The foreperson said: "We have your honor."

The judge said: "Will the defendant please stand up?" He read the paper in his hand.

The foreperson said: "We the jury find the defendant guilty of kidnapping. We however do not recommend jail time. We recommend the road of volunteer."

The judge said: "You will be doing volunteer work in Saint Peter's school and convent. If just one person comes up pregnant you will do the rest of your sentence in jail. Do you understand?"

Jean said: "Yes sir. You won't regret this."

The judge said: "See to it Jean."

CHAPTER 28

Jean started his first day of volunteer work in Saint Peter's school the very next morning. He reported to Sister Angelus' office right at 8:00 just as instructed.

Sister Angelus said: "Good morning Jean. It is nice of you to be punctual. The judge called me last night and told me to make your life miserable. We have one first grader who is incontinent. You will clean up her pee from the chair and the floor. You will clean up the vomit from the floors whenever a student gets sick. Most of them don't make it to the bathroom. You will not answer me back. Do we understand each other?"

Jean nodded his head yes. They turned out to be the best of friends over time. He even learned to like Sister Philomena. She was the one who really made him a nervous Nellie. He did manage to keep busy during the summer when the school was closed.

During that time he cleaned up the papers and the pews in the church. He had to launder the chausibles and the albs every week. They were very odoriferous in the armpit area. He laundered the nun's clothing too on Saturday. They walked around in their pajamas on Sunday morning. He was shocked to see the nuns wearing jeans on Saturday. They all did the food shopping together. He learned how to cook in those five years. Sister Philomena stayed on permanently. She did her traveling in the summer.

CHAPTER 29

An arrest was made in the state of Pennsylvania for the conviction of Jean's two accomplices. Their names were Randy and Wanda McFadden. They moved out of state and used their real names. They were extradited back to Nevada and jailed for two months while awaiting trial. They never knew about the warrant for their arrest. They left the state the day after the kidnapping. When confronted with this information they almost forgot about it. Their trial was to start the following morning. They both chose a non jury trial, which means it was the judge and the two defendants and lawyers. Trial lasted for two days.

The prosecutor and defendant lawyers were the same as for Jean's trial.

The judge said: "Peter, call your first witness please."

Peter said: "I call Randy to the stand." As Randy approached the stand he was sworn in as the witness.

Peter asked: When did you leave Nevada?"

Randy said: "We left the day after the kidnapping."

Peter asked: "Why did you leave the state?"

Randy said: "We left to escape prosecution. We also wanted to leave Jean in the lurch."

Peter asked: "Have you been in touch with Jean since you left?"

Randy said: "No. We just abandoned him."

Peter asked: "Have you tried to talk to him or call him?"

Randy said; "I just told you no."

Peter said: "No more questions your honor."

The judge said: "Paul, do you have any questions for this witness?"

Paul said: "Yes sir. Randy, who owned the guns you used?"

Randy said: "Jean did. He gave us one the day of the event."

Paul asked: "Were they registered?"

Randy said: "I don't know. He never said."

Paul said: "No more questions your honor."

The judge said: "Peter, call your first witness please."

Peter said: "I call Wanda to the stand."

As Wanda approached the stand she was sworn in as the next witness.

Peter asked; "Were your guns loaded?

Wanda said: "No. We just used them for intimidation purposes. We had no intention of harming anyone."

Peter asked: "What made you run off?"

Wanda said: "It was Sister Philomena. The way she talked to me scared me half to death. If she had a ruler she would have cracked my knuckles raw. I threw down the machine gun and high tailed it out of there."

Peter said: "No more questions your honor."

The judge said: "Very well. I am ready to enter my verdict. Will the defendants please stand?"

They both stood and the judge said: "Because it have been five years I will not put you on probation. You are ordered to return to Pennsylvania. Your names will be put into the computer system and if you so much as sneeze on a cop or look at one cross eyed you will be arrested for any reason the cop sees fit. Do you understand?"

The two defendants both nodded and said yes they understood.

The judge said: "This case is officially closed." He hammered his gavel and everybody left the court room.

When they got out of the court house both of them started breathing hard and laughing that they got away with it. They had to run very fast to get away from the cops. They took the nearest Amtrak train to Pennsylvania. They didn't care that it took 18 hours of train travel to get there. They transferred in New Mexico and then again in Chicago. Finally they arrived in Pennsylvania. They managed to live the rest of their lives out of trouble. Wanda became a bar tender and Randy became chef. They were lucky to get jobs after what they went through. Their heart stopped every time a cop car passed them in the street. For the first few months Wanda imagined they were staring at her personally. She eventually got over it though.

CHAPTER 30

At the end of the 2nd trial Robert got a phone call from Mary. She said the guard involved in the poisonings is getting released on that day. He would never work for the police department or security again. Robert was warned to be on the lookout for his name. The guard resettled in the state of Texas and became an employee at a Laundromat.

Thank you to all my faithful readers. For my next novel the group will be going to Boston, Massachusetts for a cold case to solve. They will be working with strange people and in strange places. Turn the page for the beginning excerpts already in progress.

I am sorry it doesn't have a title yet. I am just now putting together the story line. Please keep in mind that this is just the first draft. It will come out even better when it is finished.

Norman called a surprise meeting in Robert's office on March 1st. He said that he got a phone call from the Boston Police Chief and asked in there were any possibility of the group coming to Boston for a cold case. It needed fresh eyes and new ideas. Norman readily agreed to bring in himself and Robert's squad. The police chief asked if there was anything he needed. Norman said several members had cats and one member had 2 dogs. The police chief agreed to let them bring the pets and the Boston Police Department would pay for their pet friendly hotel rooms. They were also allowed to bring in their wives for a vacation. This was a surprise. John felt better about bringing along his wife and his cat. They had 2 weeks to prepare for the adventure. They rented an RV to transport their wives and pets in comfort. Mark rented his own RV because the two dogs were rather large. They needed a lot of space to stretch out.

On March 15th the caravan left Las Vegas. They took Route 80 eastbound to route 95 and then over the George Washington Bridge. Over the George Washington Bridge they went to the Major Deegan Expressway and they had to take the Cross Bronx Expressway. They went straight to Boston from there. They ran into no tolls until the GW Bridge.

They didn't even know what an EZ Pass was. Both RV's were pulled over for not having a pass and going through the EZ Pass Lane. Norman explained that they were from out of town and weren't familiar with local laws. The cops took pity on them and let them go anyway without a ticket. He gave them directions. Nobody got lost for any reason. The trip took just 2 days to drive across country. John said the meat packing trucks do this all the time. They transport hamburger meat and chicken meat and it has to get the California before it goes bad.

John asked; "Norman, what kind of mystery are we solving here?"

Norman said: "It was a 2 year old murder case where the corpse had no head, hands, or feet. There was no way of identifying the corpse."

Robert said: "It sounds like a hopeless case to solve."

Norman said: "Not for this group it isn't. I will bet my pension that by August we will have solved this case."

John asked: "Where will we be staying?"

Norman said: "We will go to the police station first and then we will get an escort to the hotel. I am told it is the Four Points Hotel in East Revere. The ladies will be doing the sightseeing and the gentlemen will be in the city of Boston working on this problem."

The front desk will tutor you in getting around the city and train system. The train system is by color coded trains. Blue, Red, Orange, Green, and Purple. The destinations are all different. There is also a Silver line. That goes to the airport. That one is free. The police department will be paying the bill for the hotel. We will also get a paycheck each week because of the extended stay. They chose the Four Points Hotel because they have a full breakfast. Because of the members of the squad being diabetic they will have an easy start to the day. The cops were sensitive to our needs.

The wives were already screeching and getting excited and cawing at each other. There was a mall right next door to the hotel.

John said: "Good God no!! They will all be broke by the end of the trip!"

Michelle and Joyce were getting excited about the idea of shopping. Food was a challenge to get to for lunch and dinner.

When they arrived at the police station everybody got out and stretched their legs. The police chief met them at the front desk. They all had to use the rest room to get freshened up. When they came out they were ready to hear the story. The 2 RV's were escorted to the hotel by 2 cops blaring their horns and lights. They arrived and were greeted by an enthusiastic hotel staff. They got to their hotel rooms and slept most of the day. John and Michelle took the cat and all his stuff out of the RV and transported them into the hotel. It took John 3 trips to finish just for the cat and the suitcases. Michelle and Joyce had rooms right next to each other. Norman and his wife and the Mark and his wife were right next to them. All four couples took over the floor. Their first task was to figure out the shower and how to operate it. Michelle had to call and ask for soap. Joyce told her never mind the soap they can get some next door at the mall. She noticed a store right next to the dentist that sold stuff like that. They also sold the soda and snacks for the evening. John and Robert never had a worry in the world about eating. Breakfast was at 7:00. The 4 couples met downstairs at 6:50. They all wanted to be the first one in line. They liked hot food and if they went later the food might not be so hot. The coffee was a little strong for their taste. They managed to get it down anyway. Norman loved it because he loved strong coffee. Joyce and Michelle didn't go back for 3rd cups. After 2 cups Michelle started to feel a little funny in the stomach area.

At 8:00 it was time for the gentlemen to leave for the first day on the job. They were met at the door by the Police Chief Himself. They were driven around for the whole summer. On the weekend John rented a car to sightsee on his own. Michelle was always afraid he would get lost. When they arrived at the police station they were taken to the jogging room in the basement. The police chief started their day out doing exercises such as jumping jacks and sit ups. They jogged in place and then jogged around the track. After 30 minutes of warm up exercises the police chief explained that his cops do this every morning to wake up their bones and muscles. They were expected to be loose and ready to run. If somebody had a big gut sticking out he would jog them in the middle of the square to embarrass them. The police chief was not allowed to put a weight limit on cops, but he could make sure they were physically fit. Some of them looked like it took them 30 minutes to get dressed in the morning. All the cops accepted this rule of being in shape and not looking embarrassing to the police department. It kept them on their toes.

After the workout the cops were taken to the chief's office to start the orientation. It was a case of a person who had no id. As near as they could tell he was a Caucasian male. His legs and privates were still in place. He was found in a park by a couple of teenagers. They called the cops because they weren't sure what they were looking at. The teenagers were given a ride home. The problem they ran into was that the original cops on the case has since passed away and they can't be questioned.

Norman said they will give it all they got.

The police chief pulled the file and the file was rather thick with incomplete notes and incomplete sentences. They could just guess how the sentences were supposed to be finished.

Meanwhile back at the hotel the ladies put together their own day's plans. The wife of the police chief came over and took over as tour guide for the first day. She promised to show them a good time and a fun day. They were very anxious to start. Their first idea was to take the hotel van to the airport road. She showed them the T subway line. It was the blue line. They took a sightseeing tour and the police chief's wife showed them the ropes on getting a pass and how to use it. They all felt rather silly. They had a picnic lunch at the grave of John Hancock. They got off at the cemetery and saw the grave stones of the original colonialists. Michelle was very much fascinated by that.

ABOUT THE AUTHOR

Wendy was born in Manhattan and attended Corpus Christi School. She also attended Mother Cabrini High School, closing in June of 2014.